STUCK

OLIVER JEFFERS

SCHOLASTIC INC.

TO THOSE WHO WERE THERE - PAPA, ROSEBUD,
DAVEBUD, THE BROTHER, THE OTHER BROTHER,
ARN, CHESTER AND SAN.

ISBN 978-0-545-60414-7

Copyright © 2011 by Oliver Jeffers.
All rights reserved. Published by Scholastic Inc.,
557 Broadway, New York, NY 10012,
by arrangement with Philomel Books, a division of Penguin Young Readers Group,
a member of Penguin Group (USA) LLC,
A Penguin Random House Company.
SCHOLASTIC and associated logos are trademarks
and/or registered trademarks of Scholastic Inc.

20 19 18 17 16   20 21 22 23 24/0

Printed in the U.S.A.   40

First Scholastic printing, April 2013

The art for *Stuck* was created by compositing various scribbles and blotches of paint,
made on small pieces of paper, all together inside my computer.
This is because I needed to move studios in the middle of making the art,
and using this approach seemed like a good idea.

IT ALL BEGAN

When Floyd's kite became stuck in A TREE.
He tried pulling and swinging, but it
WOULDN'T COME UNSTUCK.

The trouble
REALLY began

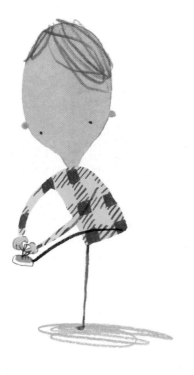

when he threw his
FAVORITE SHOE
to knock the kite loose...

...and THAT got stuck too!

So he threw up his other shoe
to knock down his FAVORITE one ...
and, UNBELievably,
that got STUCK as well.

In order to knock down
his other shoe,

Floyd fetched Mitch.

CATS get STUCK in trees
all the time, but this
WAS GETTING RIDICULOUS.

Floyd fetched
a ladder.

He was going to sort this out
once and FOR ALL...

...and up he threw it.

I'm sure you can
guess what happened.

The ladder was borrowed from a neighbor and would DEFINITELY need to be put back before anyone noticed...

and in order to do so, Floyd FLUNG a BUCKET of PAINT at it.

And wouldn't you know it... the Bucket of paint got STUCK.

Then Floyd tried...

a duck to
knock down the
bucket of paint...

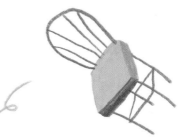

a chair
to knock down
the duck...

his friend's bicycle
to knock down
the chair...

The kitchen sink to knock down his friend's bicycle...

Floyd's front door to knock down the kitchen sink.

the FAMILY car
to knock down
their front door...

Hello?

the
MILKMAN
to knock down
the Family car...

Did you get
up here the
same way?

an orangutan to KNOCK DOWN
the milkman, who surely had
somewhere else to be...

a small boat
to knock down
the orangutan...

a BIG
BOAT
to knock
down the
small
boat...

A ~~fire~~ RhINOCEROS to knock down the BIG boat...

a long-distance TRUCK to knock down the rhinoceros...

the HOUSE across the street to knock down the long-distance TRUCK...

FLOYD?

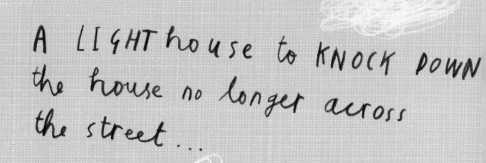

A LIGHT house to KNOCK DOWN
the house no longer across
the street...

HI!
What are
you doing?

a curious whale, in THE
WRONG PLACE at THE WRONG TIME,
to knock down the lighthouse...

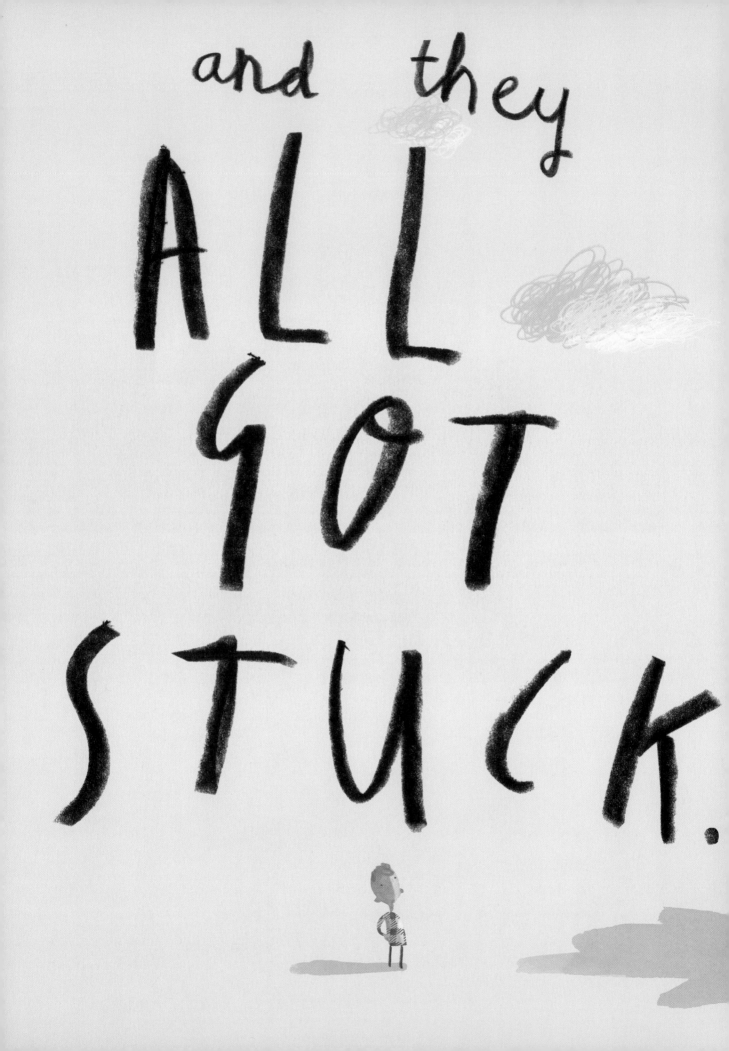

A Fire Engine was passing
and heard all the commotion.
The firemen stopped to see
if they could help at all.

And up they went...
first the engine,

followed by the firemen, one by one.

And there they stayed,
stuck between the orangutan
and one of the BOATS.

Firemen would DEFINITELY
be noticed missing, and
Floyd KNEW he'd be in
BIG TROUBLE!

Then he had
an idea,

and went to
find a SAW.

He lined it
up as best he could...

...and HURLED IT UP THE TREE.

- POP -

And that was it!
There was no more
room left in the
tree and the kite
came **unstuck**.

Floyd was delighted. He had
forgotten all about his kite
and put it to use immediately,
enjoying the rest of his DAY
very much.

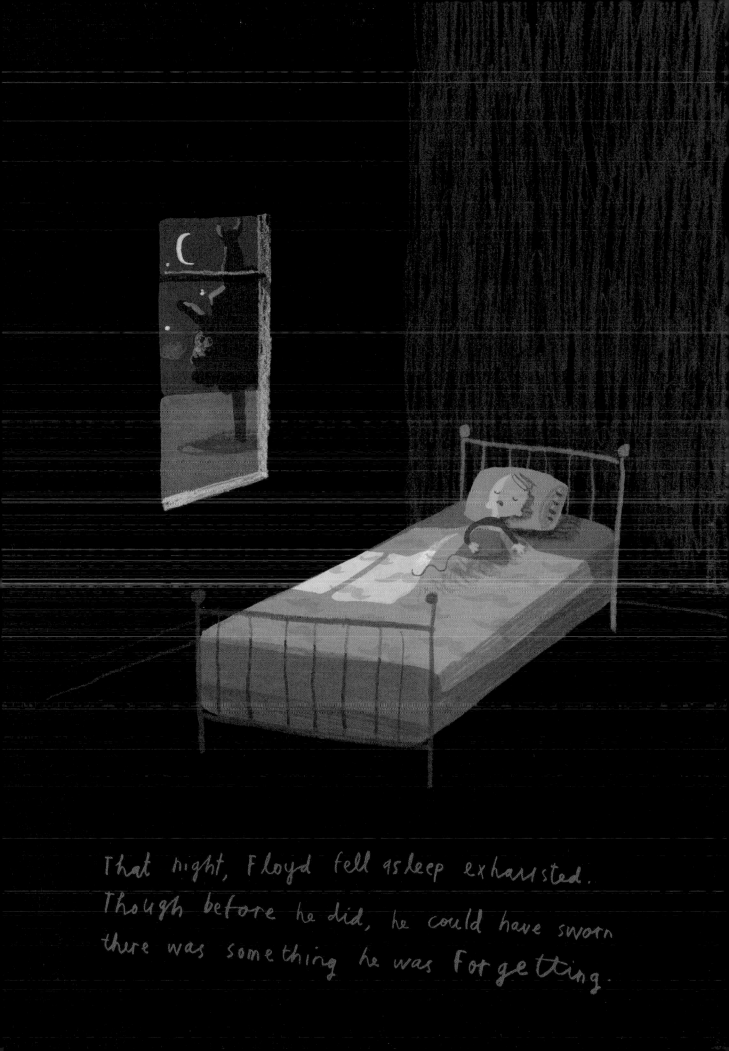

That night, Floyd fell asleep exhausted.
Though before he did, he could have sworn
there was something he was forgetting.